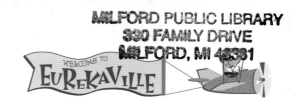

PSS!
PRICE STERN SLOAN

To Kiley and Kelsey, for all of your squeals of joy,
giggles, and curious questions—S. B.

To my wife Lois, my cat Stormy and my dog Breezy—G.C.

Text copyright © 2001 by Sylvia Branzei and Jack Keely. Illustrations copyright © 2001 by Garry Colby.
All rights reserved. Published by Price Stern Sloan, a division of Penguin Putnam Books for Young
Readers, 345 Hudson Street, New York, NY 10014. Printed in Hong Kong.
Published simultaneously in Canada. No part of this publication may be reproduced, stored in any
retrieval system, or transmitted, in any form or by any means, electronic, mechanical, photocopying,
recording or otherwise, without the prior written permission of the publisher.

Library of Congress Cataloging-in-Publication Data is available.

ISBN 0-8431-7683-0   A B C D E F G H I J

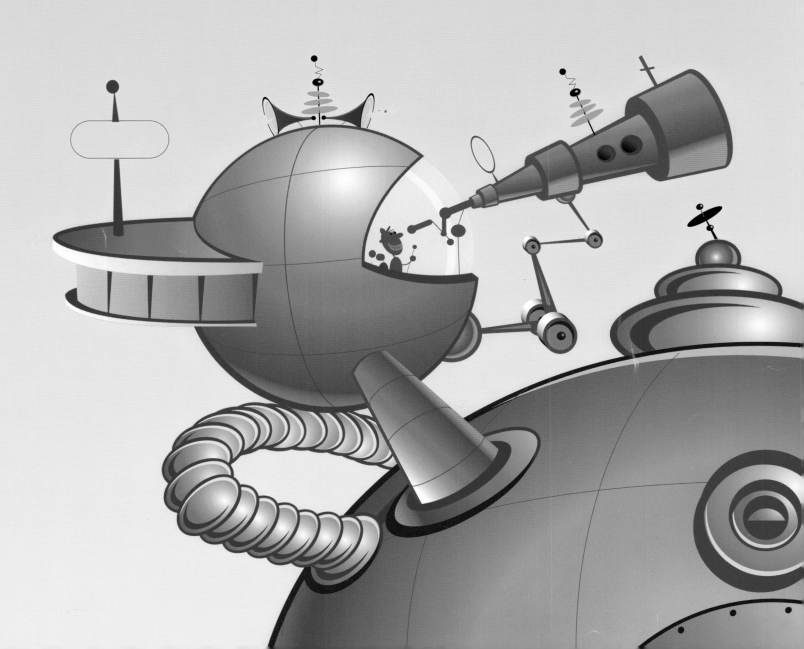

The Outer Space Place

Written by
Sylvia Branzei and **Jack Keely**

Illustrated by
Garry Colby

PSS!
PRICE STERN SLOAN

"I have hard-boiled eggs, celery, soda, pickles, and everything else we need for our picnic," said Violet. "Grab your jacket, and let's go to the park."

"Well," said Skip, "I thought we might go somewhere different for a change. Guess where?"

Violet guessed.
"The beach?
The treehouse?
The fairground?"

"No," said Skip. "OUTER SPACE!"

So Skip and Violet went to
The Outer Space Place.

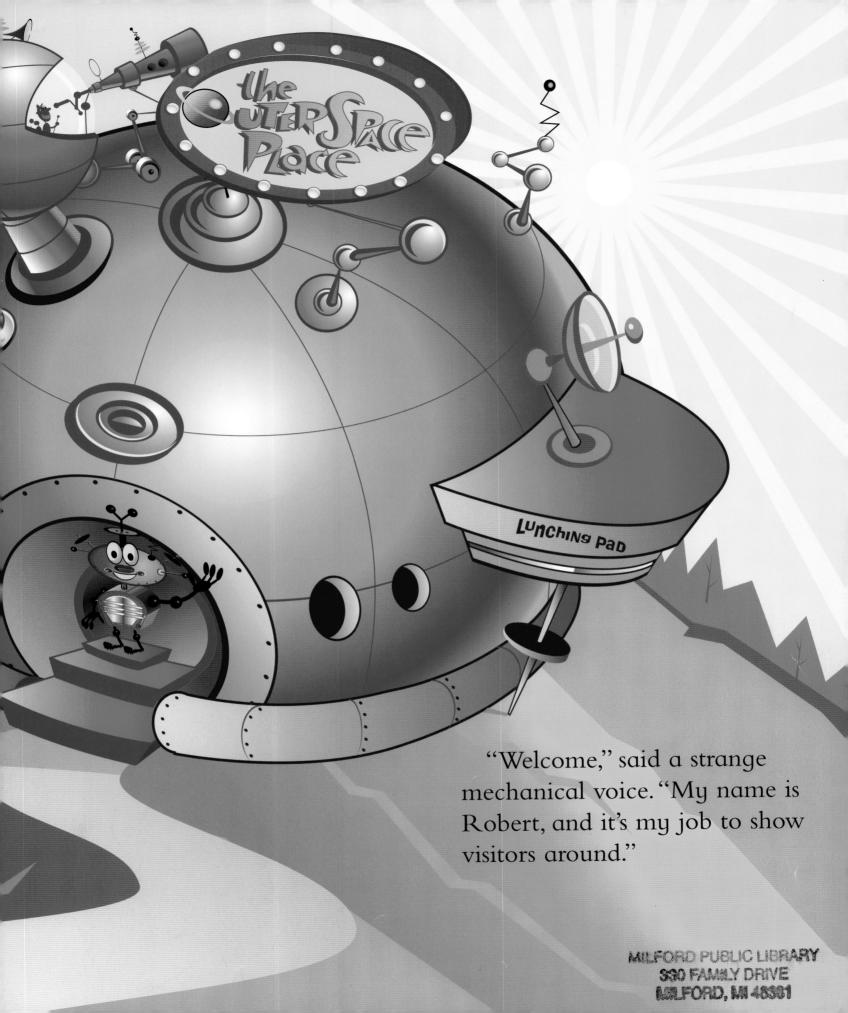

"Welcome," said a strange mechanical voice. "My name is Robert, and it's my job to show visitors around."

"We've packed a picnic, sir," said Violet.
"And we'd like to have lunch in some nice
out-of-the-way place . . . like Neptune or Mars."

"The fully automated Starsurfer VII can take you wherever you want to go," said Robert. "Just punch in your destination, and you're on your way. You'll need special suits to walk around on distant worlds. Outer space is very different from Eurekaville."

"Look! The moon!" shouted Violet. "Let's stop there."

"Oh, lots of people have been there already. Let's go someplace new," said Skip. "We don't have enough to share with the Man in the Moon. Besides, I don't like green cheese."

"The moon isn't made of green cheese, silly. That's as dopey as thinking there are flying saucers. And there's no Man in the Moon, either. People just think they see a face—it's really craters and rocks."

MOON

Gravity from Earth keeps you
(and the moon) from floating away.
Gravity from the moon causes high
and low tides on Earth.

The moon is Earth's
nearest neighbor.
It's "only" 240,000
miles away.

In 1969, the first man
landed on the moon.

"I know, Violet," said Skip. "Picnics are fun in the sun.
Let's stop there and catch some rays."

"We can't land on the sun! It's a star," explained Violet.
"Stars are balls of burning gases."

"Wow, talk about sunburn," said Skip. "By the way,
are you sure you don't believe in flying saucers?"

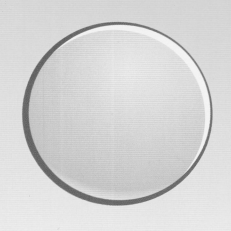

"How 'bout a planet? Let's go someplace nearby for lunch . . . like Mercury!" said Skip.

"One side of Mercury always faces the sun!" said Violet. "It would be like sitting inside a furnace. And on the side that faces away, it drops to three hundred degrees below zero!"

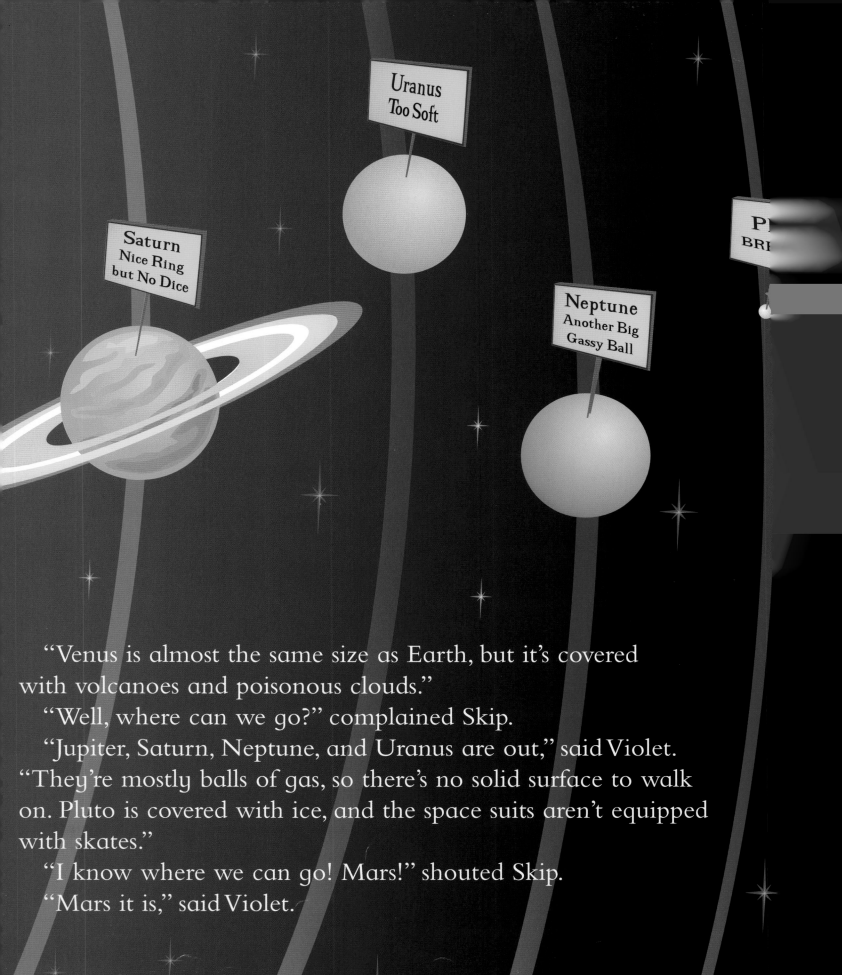

"Venus is almost the same size as Earth, but it's covered
with volcanoes and poisonous clouds."

"Well, where can we go?" complained Skip.

"Jupiter, Saturn, Neptune, and Uranus are out," said Violet.
"They're mostly balls of gas, so there's no solid surface to walk
on. Pluto is covered with ice, and the space suits aren't equipped
with skates."

"I know where we can go! Mars!" shouted Skip.

"Mars it is," said Violet.

"Well, here we are, Skip. How do you like Mars?"

"It's just a rocky red desert. Where are the Martian canals? Where are the little green men?"

"Those are just legends," answered Violet. "I think Mars is fascinating."

"It's okay, I guess. But it's not very exciting," said Skip. "Let's go farther out in space, and see what we can find."

Mars is red because of rust in its soil.

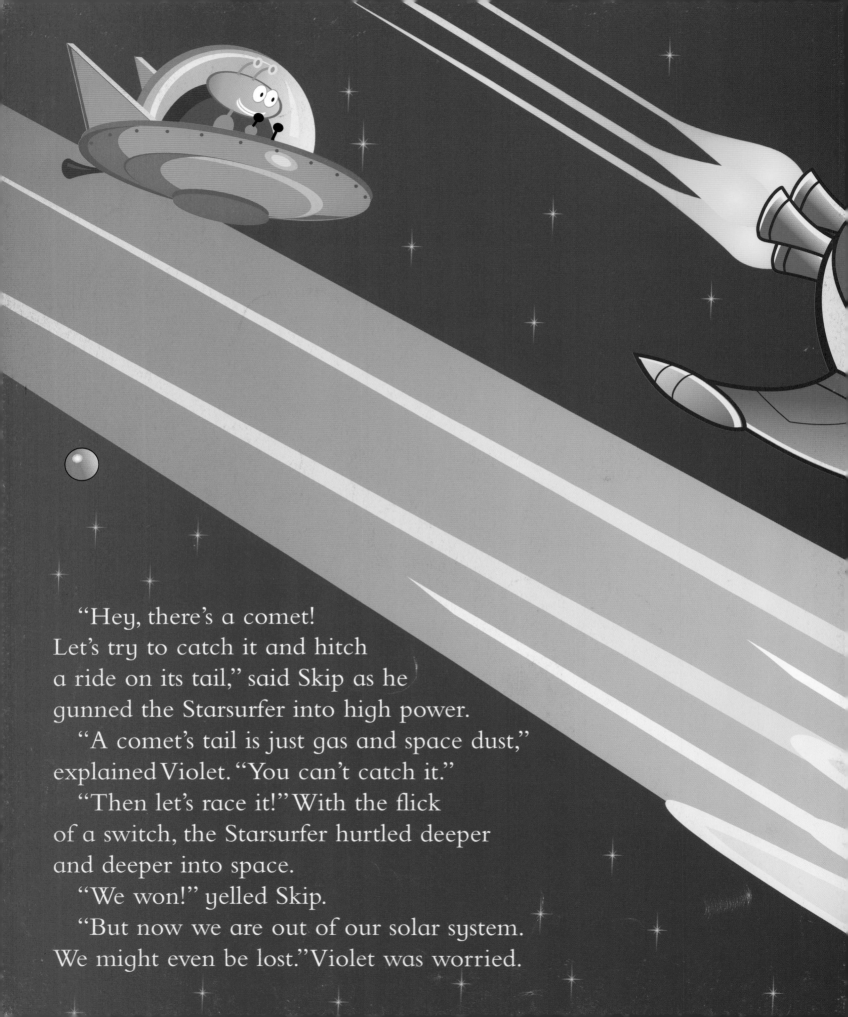

"Hey, there's a comet!
Let's try to catch it and hitch
a ride on its tail," said Skip as he
gunned the Starsurfer into high power.

"A comet's tail is just gas and space dust,"
explained Violet. "You can't catch it."

"Then let's race it!" With the flick
of a switch, the Starsurfer hurtled deeper
and deeper into space.

"We won!" yelled Skip.

"But now we are out of our solar system.
We might even be lost." Violet was worried.

In ancient times, people feared comets. They thought a comet meant something really bad was about to happen.

Comets travel in regular orbits around the sun . . . just like the Earth does.

Halley's Comet comes by like clockwork— every 76 years.

Skip heard a *ping* sound as something streaked past the ship.

"Hey, someone threw a rock at us!" Skip said.

"It was a meteoroid, and here come some more!" gasped Violet. "You'd better do some fancy steering, Skip."

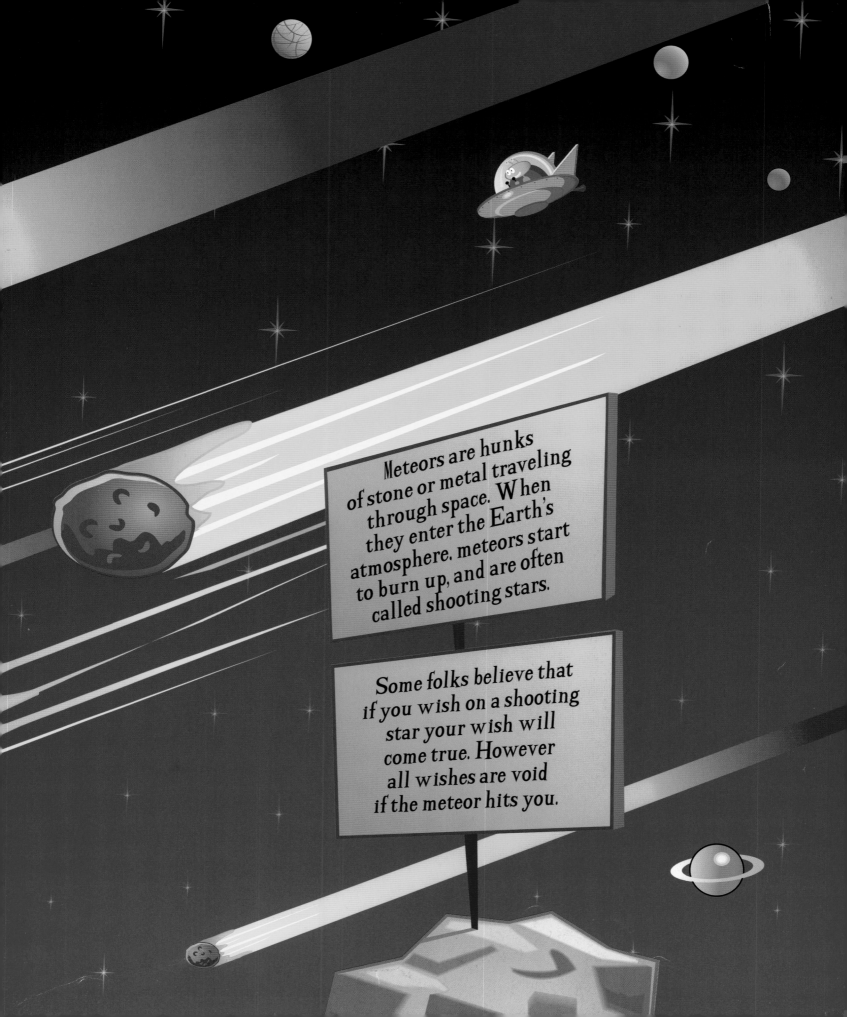

Meteors are hunks of stone or metal traveling through space. When they enter the Earth's atmosphere, meteors start to burn up, and are often called shooting stars.

Some folks believe that if you wish on a shooting star your wish will come true. However all wishes are void if the meteor hits you.

When they were out of range of the flying rocks,
Violet sighed with relief.

"So, that's a meteor shower," laughed Skip.
"How fun! We should turn around and do it again."

"Oh no," screamed Violet. "We're heading into a black hole!
The gravity in a black hole is so strong that nothing can escape it.
Put the ship into reverse, FAST!"

EEEEEeeeeeeerrrrrrmmmmm. Swoosh.

Gravity on a black hole is so strong that it sucks in anything near it, including light. That's why it's called a black hole.

They occur when stars burn out and collapse in on themselves.

"That was close. I'm not sure how we managed to escape that old black hole," said Violet. "Where to now?"

"I just want to go home," said Skip. "We've been hurled all over the universe and still haven't had lunch!"

"Ahhhh, there's Eurekaville," said Skip.
"I see the Outer Space Place. All clear
for a landing."

"Skip, let's stop at the galactic gift shop
after we return the Starsurfer VII. I have
an idea."

"This is perfect," said Skip.
"Thank you and come again," said Robert.

"Now we can visit outer space anytime," said Skip.

"You said it, Spaceman," said Violet. "And we don't even need to leave the ground!"